PANTHEON

PANTHEON

••VOLUME I: HETEROTOPIA••

STORY AND ART BY
AWET MOGES

EDITOR AND
CONTRIBUTING WRITER
DAVID MISIALOWSKI

INTERIOR COLOR BOOKS 1 AND 3:
SAJID MOHAMMED, SAFEEZSTUDIO@GMAIL.COM
INTERIOR COLOR BOOKS 2 AND 4:
MARIANOVELLA SINICROPI AND NICOLE SERRA
INTERIOR COLOR BOOK 5:
CARMIN LOPEZ
INTERIOR FRONT SPLASH PAGE COLOR:
DAVID DELANTY

ISBN 10: 1-944854-04-5
ISBN 13: 978-1-944854-04-1

www.poodpawprints.com
facebook.com/poodpawprints

CHAPTER ONE

PANTHEON: HETEROTOPIA CHAPTER ONE

WHAT IS PANTHEON? THE PROSIAC ANSWER: AN EPIC TALE WITH PHILOSOPHICAL CHARACTERS FROM MYTHOLOGY SET IN A POSTHUMAN FUTURE. IF THAT FAILS TO PIQUE YOUR INTEREST, HOW ABOUT THIS SLIGHTLY MORE ESOTERIC ANSWER:

PANTHEON IS THEORY-FICTION MASQUERADING AS A GRAPHIC NOVEL, IN WHICH THE VAPORS OF THE GOLDEN AGE WAFT OUT AND CLOT INTO A HERETICAL CYNICISM THAT SAVAGES ITSELF AS A PERVERSE SLAVE OF ITS OWN EXISTENTIAL NIHILISM. PANTHEON GNAWS AT THE ROOT OF THE YGGDRASIL OF ITS OWN FATUOUS ABORTION, WITH AN AMPUTATED MYTHOS THAT GOOSE-STEPS AROUND PETRIFIED TOTEMS OF EXHAUSTED POP ART, EITHER OUT OF MOCKERY OR PERVERSION.

TOO RICH? SUFFICE IT TO SAY THAT IN MYTHOLOGY, THE GODS PUNISH HUBRIS BY IMPOSING FRUSTRATION -- ALLOW A MORTAL TO ALMOST ACHIEVE HER DESIRES ONLY TO BE DENIED IN THE END.

IN PANTHEON, THE FATES PUNISH NAIVETE BY IMOSING EXISTENTIAL FAILURE -- ALLOW A GODDESS TO ACHIEVE HER GOALS ONLY TO BE DISAPPOINTED IN THE END.

ROLL ON THOU DEEP AND DARK BLUE OCEAN, ROLL! TEN THOUSAND FLEETS SWEEP OVER THEE IN VAIN; MAN MARKS THE EARTH WITH HIS RUIN - HIS CONTROL STOPS WITH THE SHORE. --BYRON

BEHOLD A WORTHY SIGHT, TO WHICH THE GOD, TURNING HIS ATTENTION TO HIS OWN WORK, MAY DIRECT HIS GAZE. BEHOLD AN EQUAL THING, WORTHY OF A GOD, A BRAVE MAN MATCHED IN CONFLICT WITH EVIL FORTUNE. -- SENECA

THE CYCLE OF THE OCEAN GROWS AND FLEES AGAINST THE OCCULT PULL OF DIANA'S SILVERY ORB, SERVING AS A REMINDER OF THE IMMORTAL EYE OF RE, WHAT MAN ONCE EVOKED, "DIVINE!"

SLABS OF LIMESTONE THAT STOOD FOR MILLIONS OF YEARS HAVE STARTED TO CRUMBLE UNDER THE RELENTLESS POUNDING OF THE OCEAN, THE PULL OF THE TIDE AS IT WHETS SMOOTH THE JAGGED CORNERS OF MIGHTY CLIFFS.

A CONSTANT STRUGGLE FOR DOMINANCE, THE SEA AND LAND BOTH EXERT THEIR WILL TO POWER IN AN ETERNAL DANCE STEP.

THE BUBBLING FROTH OF THE OCEAN, AS IT CARESSES THE ANCIENT MARL, SNAKES AMONG HER TOES. HERE LIES A WOMAN OF PULCHRITUDE, POSSESSING A FEROCIOUS BEAUTY, A JEWEL POSEIDON OF OLD DISCARDED AS IF TO BOAST OF HIS GENEROSITY. O FORLORN SOLITUDE!

HOVERING ABOVE THE SPRAWLING FIGURE A FLEETING SHADE FLICKERS & BRIEFLY BLOTS OUT THE UNFORGIVING MORNING SUN. A PIERCING CRY SHATTERS THE TRANQUILITY & REPEATS. THE PRICKLY CAW SEEMS TO HERALD THE BIRTH OF A NEW DAY UPON THE SILENT COAST.

ANIMATION IS BORN! JERKING LIMBS & A COLD SHUDDER RUDELY INTRODUCE HER TO A SEARING PAIN IN HER THROAT.

BLAARRGH!!!

DISGUSTING... MY HEAD BURNS.. WATER... SALT WATER... TOO MUCH SALT.

THE CROW STRETCHES ITS WINGS, SHAKES OFF THE MORNING DEW, AND LIGHTS UPON THE SHEER EASTERN WALL OF THE CLIFF.

VOMITING THE SILT & SALT OF THE OCEAN, SHE DISGORGES THE CONTENTS OF HER BELLY, & EMPTIES THE AIR OF HER LUNGS.

WATER? AN OCEAN? A BEACH? WHERE AM I? WHO AM I?

ATOP THE LIMESTONE CLIFF, STRETCHING VASTLY OUT BEFORE HER &
SHIMMERING IN THE MORNING SUNLIGHT LIKE A PHANTASM, LIKE A
FEVER DREAM, IS A TITANIC GEOMETRICAL STRUCTURE, A TEMPLE OR A
MAUSOLEUM, THE INTRICATE DESIGN OF WHICH MOCKS THE CHAOS
OF HER UPROOTED REBIRTH FROM AN UNREMEMBERED PAST.

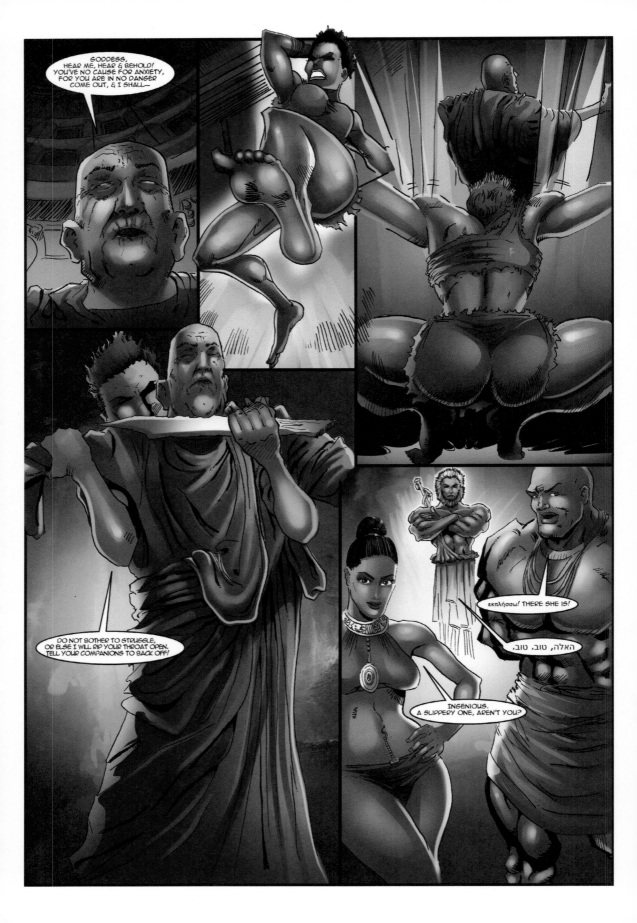

...THE NEXUS!

IT IS THE GATEWAY TO THE
MULTIWORLDS OF THE MYTHOSCAPE.
ITS POLISHED, REFLECTIVE SILVER SURFACE
IS ACTUALLY A FILAMENT OF *HYPERSPACETIME*
THAT'S EXACTLY *ONE PLANCK LENGTH THICK.*

THE NEXUS RECREATES THE
SINGULARITY AT THE TIME OF THE
CREATION, WHEN ALL TIME WAS THE
SAME TIME, ALL SPACE THE SAME
SPACE, & ALL MODALITY THE SAME
MODALITY: ALL WAS ONE, &
ONE WAS ALL.

THROUGH IT ONE MAY TESSERACT
INTO HIGHER DIMENSIONS OR VISIT PARALLEL
WORLDS – ALTERNATIVE VERSIONS OF REALITY.

ONE MAY PASS INSTANTANEOUSLY
THROUGH VAST VISTAS OF SPACE & TIME,
HOPSCOTCHING ACROSS THE UNIVERSE.

PANTHEON
HETEROTOPIA

CHAPTER TWO

Pantheon: Heterotopia Chapter Two

A goddess adrift on a dead sea has washed up on a barren land. Her memory is as empty as the world. Presided over by an enigmatic crow or raven, she climbs a vertiginous escarpment and, at the summit, is dazzled and dumfounded by what lies on the other side: a mighty temple. Exploring inside, she is ambushed by — or ambushes — a retinue of gods & an Ancient, paternalistic entity called Cartaphilus. This is Team Pantheon. They show her the museum over which they preside: It houses the religious totems, relics and artifacts of a vanished humanity, a species that has departed from the scene for reasons obscure. Among these artifacts is the hammer of Thor. The amnesiac Goddess grabs the hammer and smites two of the team's foes — and learns by stages that these gods are grooming her. For what?

Call me Kaeli, she tells them, though she still knows not who she really is.

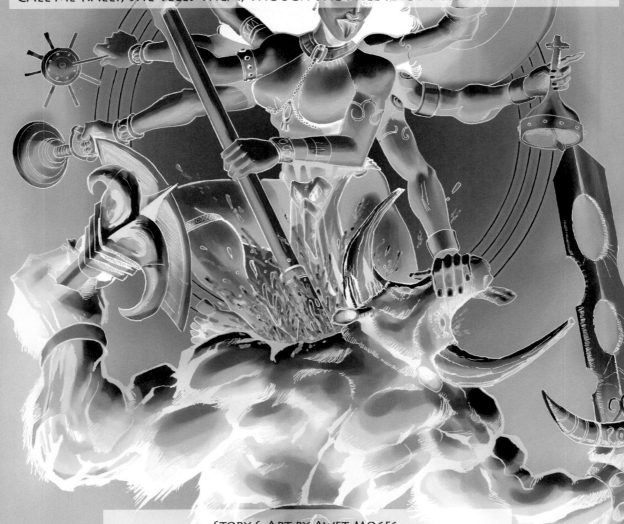

Story & Art by Awet Moges
Editor and Contributing Writer: David Misialowski
Cover colors by Sajid Mohammed
Interior colors by Marianovella Sinicropi & Nicole Serra

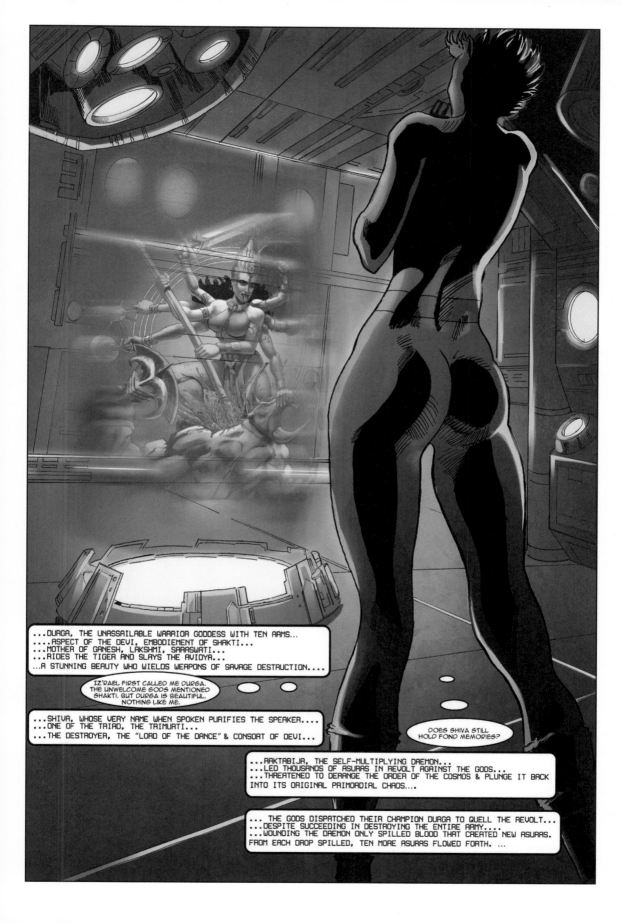

...DURGA, THE UNASSAILABLE WARRIOR GODDESS WITH TEN ARMS...
....ASPECT OF THE DEVI, EMBODIEMENT OF SHAKTI...
...MOTHER OF GANESH, LAKSHMI, SARASWATI...
...RIDES THE TIGER AND SLAYS THE AVIDYA...
...A STUNNING BEAUTY WHO WIELDS WEAPONS OF SAVAGE DESTRUCTION....

IZ'RAEL FIRST CALLED ME DURGA.
THE UNWELCOME GODS MENTIONED
SHAKTI. BUT DURGA IS BEAUTIFUL.
NOTHING LIKE ME.

...SHIVA, WHOSE VERY NAME WHEN SPOKEN PURIFIES THE SPEAKER....
...ONE OF THE TRIAD, THE TRIMURTI...
...THE DESTROYER, THE "LORD OF THE DANCE" & CONSORT OF DEVI...

DOES SHIVA STILL
HOLD FOND MEMORIES?

...RAKTABIJA, THE SELF-MULTIPLYING DAEMON...
...LED THOUSANDS OF ASURAS IN REVOLT AGAINST THE GODS...
...THREATENED TO DERANGE THE ORDER OF THE COSMOS & PLUNGE IT BACK
INTO ITS ORIGINAL PRIMORDIAL CHAOS....

... THE GODS DISPATCHED THEIR CHAMPION DURGA TO QUELL THE REVOLT...
...DESPITE SUCCEEDING IN DESTROYING THE ENTIRE ARMY....
...WOUNDING THE DAEMON ONLY SPILLED BLOOD THAT CREATED NEW ASURAS.
FROM EACH DROP SPILLED, TEN MORE ASURAS FLOWED FORTH. ...

AY, THERE'S THE RUB. TOTAL RECALL MAY EVEN *DEEPEN* YOUR ANXIETY. YOUR EPIPHANY MAY FLAME OUT INTO THE ASHES OF DESPAIR.

MAYBE. BUT I CANNOT LET THAT STOP ME. I MUST TAKE THE RISK BECAUSE I *HATE* BEING AT A DISADVANTAGE, BEING UNSURE, CONSTANTLY QUESTIONING MY OWN MOTIVES.

I NEED TO KNOW *WHO* & *WHAT* I REALLY AM.

WOULDN'T YOU WANT TO KNOW THE SAME, IF YOU WALKED IN MY SHOES?

WELL... I DON'T KNOW. MY LIFE HAS BEEN A LONG SERIES OF TRAGIC COMEDIES. BUT AGAIN, I WANT TO CAUTION YOU AGAINST HOPING FOR TOO MUCH. THE DESIRE FOR SALVATION MAY, IF REALIZED, PERVERSELY YIELD THE OPPOSITE RESULT: *DAMNATION.*

SALVATION & DAMNATION ARE TWO SIDES OF THE SAME COIN, THE *YIN & YANG.*

JUST AS WITH THE MORTALS OVER WHOM WE ONCE RULED. WHAT HAPPENED TO THEM?

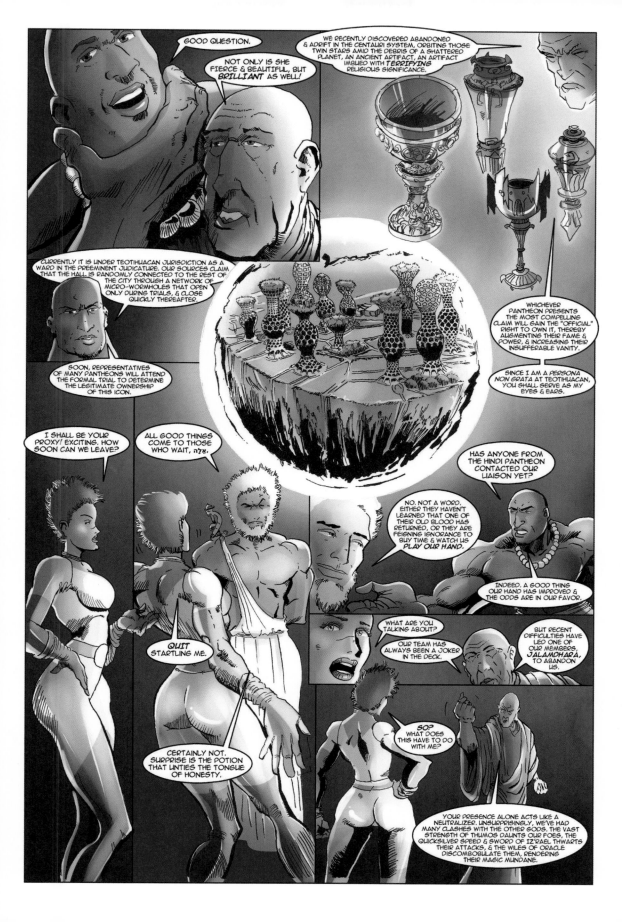

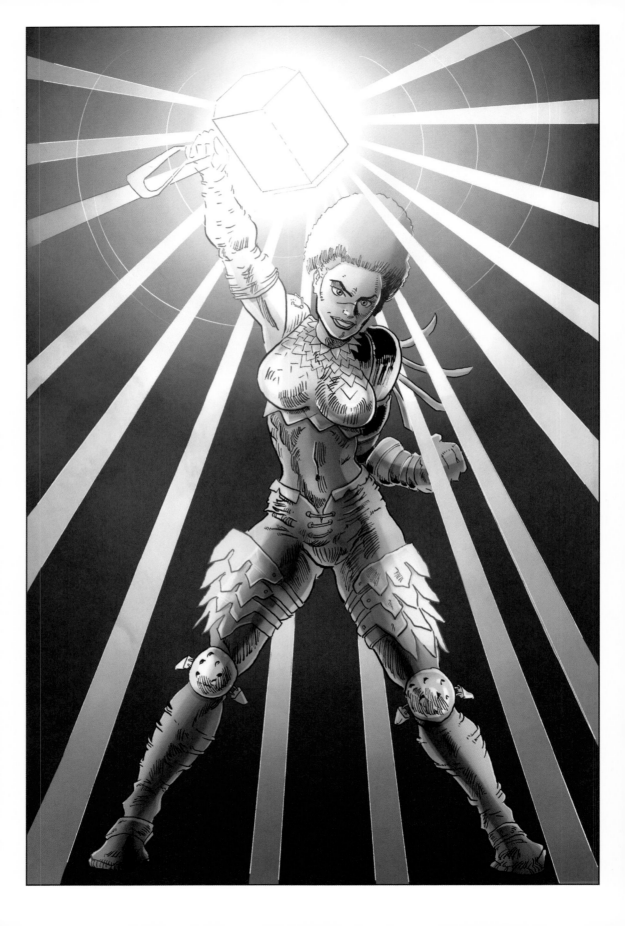

HETEROTOPIA
CHAPTER THREE

PANTHEON: HETEROTOPIA CHAPTER THREE

KAELI STRUGGLES TO REUNITE WITH THE MOTHER THAT HAS ABANDONED HER, THE MOTHER NAMED MEMORY. WHAT WILL SHE FIND IF SHE DISCOVERS WHO SHE REALLY IS? SALVATION? DESTRUCTION? PERHAPS BOTH? IN THE MEANTIME SHE LEARNS WHAT TEAM PANTHEON REALLY WANTS & WHAT IT WAGES; WAR ON WORSHIP ITSELF.

TO THAT END THEY SEIZE, IMPRISON & DEACTIVATE THE MYTHOFACTS OF WORSHIP: THE CROSSES & CRESCENTS, THE TABERNACLES & TOTEMS, ALL THAT BEFORE WHICH MORTALS BOW & CRAWL, GROVEL & GENUFLECT. FOR ACROSS THE FAR-FLUNG COSMOS REMAIN MANY MORTALS WHO ARE NOT MEN, BUT LIKE MEN THEY ARE ADDICTED TO GOD WORSHIP.

SHE LEARNS THAT CARTAPHILUS, THE LEADER OF THE TEAM, IS THE LAST REMAINING MAN, AN IMMORTAL MORTAL. AND THEY RECRUIT KAELI FOR A MISSION, A SOJOURN TO THE TEOTIHLIACAN, THE CITY OF THE GODS. THEIR GOAL IS TO CONFISCATE AN ANCIENT ARTIFACT IMBUED WITH TERRIFYING RELIGIOUS SIGNIFICANCE.

KAELI INSISTS THAT ON THIS MISSION SHE BE ALLOWED TO KEEP THOR'S HAMMER, FOR IT INFUSES HER WITH THE POWER & CONFIDENCE THAT SHE — AS AN ORPHAN OF MOTHER MEMORY — STILL LACKS. THOUGH THE REACTIVATION OF THE HAMMER CONTRAVENES THE GOAL OF DISARMING IT, THE TEAM GRUDGINGLY ACCEDES TO HER DEMAND.

NOW IT'S OFF TO THE CITY OF THE GODS!

STORY & ART BY AWET MOGES
EDITOR AND CONTRIBUTING WRITER: DAVID MISIALOWSKI
COVER COLORS BY MARIANOVELLA SINICROPI
INTERIOR COLORS BY SAJID MOHAMMED

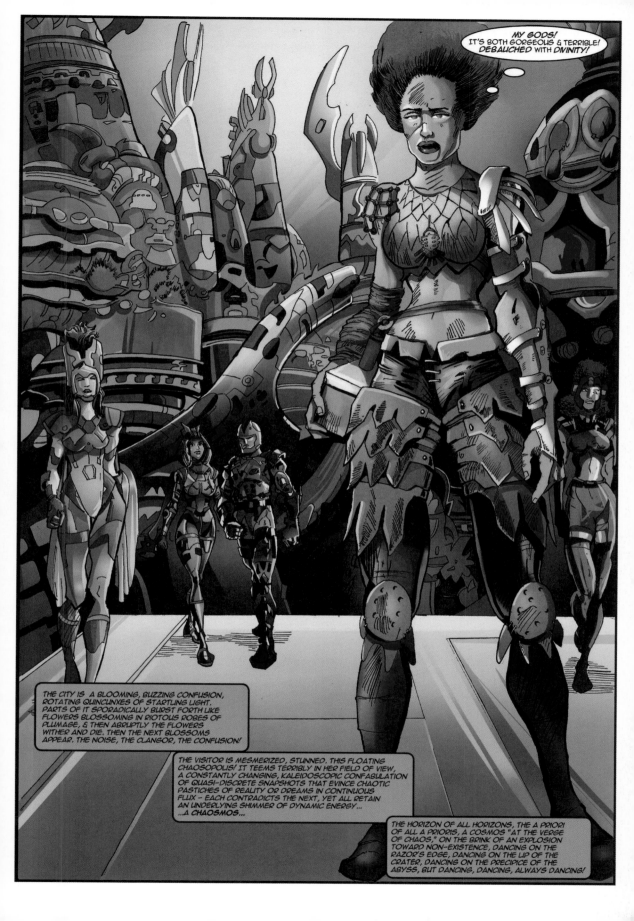

MY GODS!
IT'S BOTH GORGEOUS & TERRIBLE!
DEBAUCHED WITH DIVINITY!

THE CITY IS A BLOOMING, BUZZING CONFUSION,
ROTATING QUINCUNXES OF STARTLING LIGHT.
PARTS OF IT SPORADICALLY BURST FORTH LIKE
FLOWERS BLOSSOMING IN RIOTOUS ROBES OF
PLUMAGE, & THEN ABRUPTLY THE FLOWERS
WITHER AND DIE. THEN THE NEXT BLOSSOMS
APPEAR. THE NOISE, THE CLANGOR, THE CONFUSION!

THE VISITOR IS MESMERIZED, STUNNED. THIS FLOATING
CHAOSOPOLIS! IT TEEMS TERRIBLY IN HER FIELD OF VIEW,
A CONSTANTLY CHANGING, KALEIDOSCOPIC CONFABULATION
OF QUASI-DISCRETE SNAPSHOTS THAT EVINCE CHAOTIC
PASTICHES OF REALITY OR DREAMS IN CONTINUOUS
FLUX – EACH CONTRADICTS THE NEXT, YET ALL RETAIN
AN UNDERLYING SHIMMER OF DYNAMIC ENERGY...
...A CHAOSMOS...

THE HORIZON OF ALL HORIZONS, THE A PRIORI
OF ALL A PRIORIS, A COSMOS "AT THE VERGE
OF CHAOS," ON THE BRINK OF AN EXPLOSION
TOWARD NON-EXISTENCE, DANCING ON THE
RAZOR'S EDGE, DANCING ON THE LIP OF THE
CRATER, DANCING ON THE PRECIPICE OF THE
ABYSS, BUT DANCING, DANCING, ALWAYS DANCING!

THE CONGREGATION OF DEITIES IS A
RICH CORNUCOPIA FOR THE NEWCOMER.
WHAT SPLENDID ENTITIES! SUCH MARVELOUS
COUNTENANCES! EACH IS MORE POWERFUL &
PROFOUND THAN THE OTHER, WHICH
PARADOXICALLY MEANS THAT NONE IS BETTER
THAN ANY THOUGH EACH IS THE BEST.

THEY SPEECHIFY ELOQUENTLY &
GESTICULATE DRAMATICALLY, IN A
DIFFERENT BUT LONG-LOST ERA, &
WERE THEY MORTALS, THEY WOULD
HAVE BEEN MEMBERS OF THE ROMAN
SENATE PREENING ON C-SPAN.
IN SUM, THEY HAVE GRAVITAS.

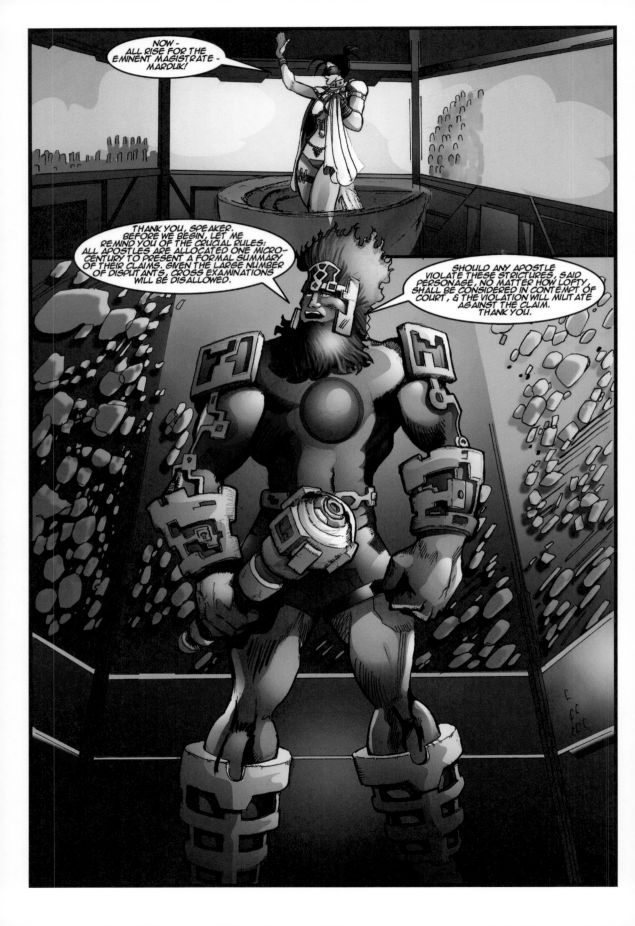

GREETINGS, MY FELLOW DIVINITIES! I SPEAK FOR THE SERAPHIM, & NEED ONLY DECLARE THE TRUE IDENTITY OF THE OBJECT UNDER QUESTION IN ORDER TO STATE OUR UNDENIABLE CLAIM IN FULL. THE ARTIFACT HAS BEEN DETERMINED TO BE THE LONG LOST *HOLY CHALICE* – THE VERY CUP THAT OUR LORD & SAVIOR JESUS CHRIST BLESSED AT THE *LAST SUPPER*, "WHOSOEVER DRINKETH THIS CUP SHALL HAVE EVERLASTING LIFE..." EVEN THOUGH THIS GRAL HAS BEEN BURIED FOR EONS UNDER THE BURDENSOME LANDSLIDE OF LEGEND AND MYTH, IT RECENTLY RESURFACED DURING THE *HOLY MISSION* OF THE ESTEEMED NIMROD IN THE CENTAURI SYSTEM. IPSO FACTO, THIS SACRED ICON BELONGS TO *US*, THE SOLE REMAINING REPRESENTATIVES OF CHRISTIANITY, AND MUST BE RETURNED TO US FORTHWITH. THANK YOU.

I REPRESENT THE GODS OF THE *CENTAURIANS*. OUR PANTHEON HAS AN INALIENABLE RIGHT – TECHNICALLY A *PROPRIETARY* RIGHT – TO THIS ARTIFACT, BECAUSE IT WAS FOUND IN OUR PRECINCTS. OUR WORSHIPERS HAVE ALREADY EMBRACED THIS ICON AS THE VERY *SYMBOL* OF IMMORTALITY. THERE IS NOTHING TO DEBATE HERE. TO THE EXTENT THAT WE DO DEBATE, WE DO SO ONLY OUT OF *MAGNANIMITY*. WE CONFIDENTLY SUBMIT OUR FAITH IN THE RIGHTNESS OF OUR CLAIM TO THE *WISDOM* OF THE *FATES*, NO DOUBT THEY WILL PRONOUNCE THE CORRECT DECISION: THE ONLY *POSSIBLE* DECISION: WHERE THE ICON WAS FOUND, IS WHERE IT IS MEANT TO BE.

I OFFER NO ELABORATE SPEECH, & I HAVE NO INTEREST IN THE CHALICE. I NEED ONLY STATE THE OBVIOUS: THE POTENTIAL ENRICHMENT OF KNOWLEDGE THAT THIS ARTIFACT WOULD BRING UNDER THE COLD, CLINICAL & DISINTERESTED EYE OF THE *MAGI*. THUS, I PROPOSE WARDING IT TO THE SCIENTISTS, THE ARCHAEOLOGISTS, THE PHILOSOPHERS. IT HAS BEEN THE *CORNUCOPIA* FOR THE OLYMPIANS, UNTIL TYCHE LOST IT, & THE *CAULDRON* OF THE TUATHA DE DANAAN, & ILMARINEN'S *SAMPO*. THE JURY ALREADY POSSESSES THE NECESSARY WISDOM THAT TO REJECT ALL DIVINE CLAIMS TO THIS GRAL IS TO ACKNOWLEDGE THE INCONGRUENCE BETWEEN DECLARED NOBLE INTENTIONS & HIDDEN MOTIVATIONS OF A POLITICAL NATURE.

THIS DAMNED SANCTIFIED CUP? I PROPOSE THE RADICAL SOLUTION OF *DESTROYING IT*. THIS ARTIFACT IS THE *GOLDEN APPLE* OF ERIS, A *TROJAN HORSE*, & THE PANTHEON THAT WINS IT WILL HAVE ACHIEVED A PYRRHIC VICTORY. ITS PROMISE OF POWER WILL DO NAUGHT BUT SPLINTER THE FRAGILE ALLIANCES BETWEEN THE PANTHEONS, DROP A THUMB ON THE SCALES OF JUSTICE & SPELL THE CATACLYSMIC END OF OUR ERA. THE FLUID FUTURE REMAINS OURS TO MOLD, UNTIL IT IS TOO LATE & OSSIFIES INTO THE PAST. THIS CHALICE MUST BE DESTROYED, AS WAS ITS PROGENITOR IN A BATH OF BLOOD. *DESTROY IT!!!*

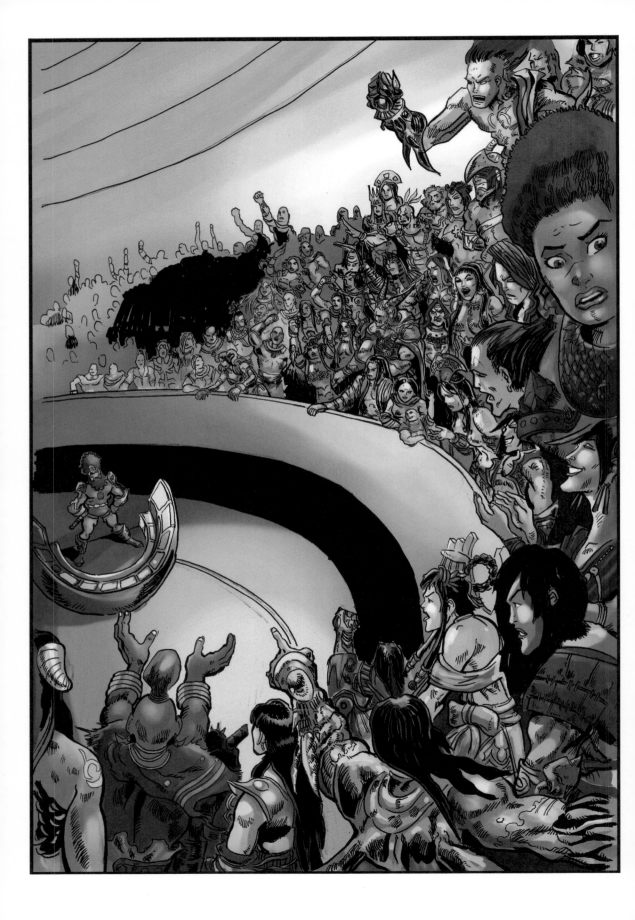

PANTHEON

HETEROTOPIA
CHAPTER FOUR

KAELI HAS ARRIVED IN THE CITY OF THE GODS, AND IS AGOG. A STUPEFYING
CHAOSMOS! SHE RESOLVES TO BLEND IN AND WOO AND WIN ALLIES. SHE LEARNS
HINTS TO HER PAST IN THE REACTION OF THE VARIOUS DEITIES TO HER NAME. THE
GOD THOTH, HER PERSONAL ESCORT, DEMYSTIFIES THE GREAT COSMOPOLIS FOR HER.
DESPITE ITS SPLENDOR, IT IS A DYSFUNCTIONAL DYSTOPIA, PRESIDED OVER BY
BUNGLING BUREAUCRATS AND MYTHODEMONIC DEMIURGES.

ALL THE GODS AND GODDESSES ARE HERE FOR THE TRIAL, WHEREIN OWNERSHIP OF
THE RENEGADE MYTHOFACT, IMBUED WITH SUCH PROFOUND POWER, WILL BE ADJU-
DICATED. THE OBJECT AT WARRANT IS THE VENERABLE HOLY GRAIL. CLAIMS AND
COUNTERCLAIMS ARE MADE BEFORE A JURY, A DEPUTATION OF ELDERS. BUT IT IS JUST
A SHOW TRIAL, FOR IN REALITY THE MOIRAE, THE THREE SISTERS OF FATE, DECIDE.
THEY DECLARE A MISTRIAL, LEAVING THE GRAIL IN LIMBO.

OUTRAGE AND CONFUSION WASH OVER THIS CONVOCATION OF DIVINE VANITIES —
DIVANITIES, TO COIN A NEOLOGISM. WITH KAELI'S GREAT MALLET SERVING AS A DIS-
TRACTION — FOR ALL EYES ARE ON IT RATHER THAN THE CHALICE — TEAM
PANTHEON ABSCONDS WITH THE MIGHTY MYTHOFACT. LEAVING BEHIND A DECOY
CHALICE TO BUY TIME, THE TEAM FLEES WITH ITS PRIZE — ONLY TO DISCOVER THAT
NOW THEY ARE THE HUNTED, RATHER THAN THE HUNTERS.

THE CHASE IS ON!

STORY AND ART AWET MOGES
EDITOR AND CONTRIBUTING WRITER: DAVID MISIALOWSKI
COVER COLORS BY MARIANOVELLA SINICROPI
INTERIOR COLORS BY NICOLE SERRA

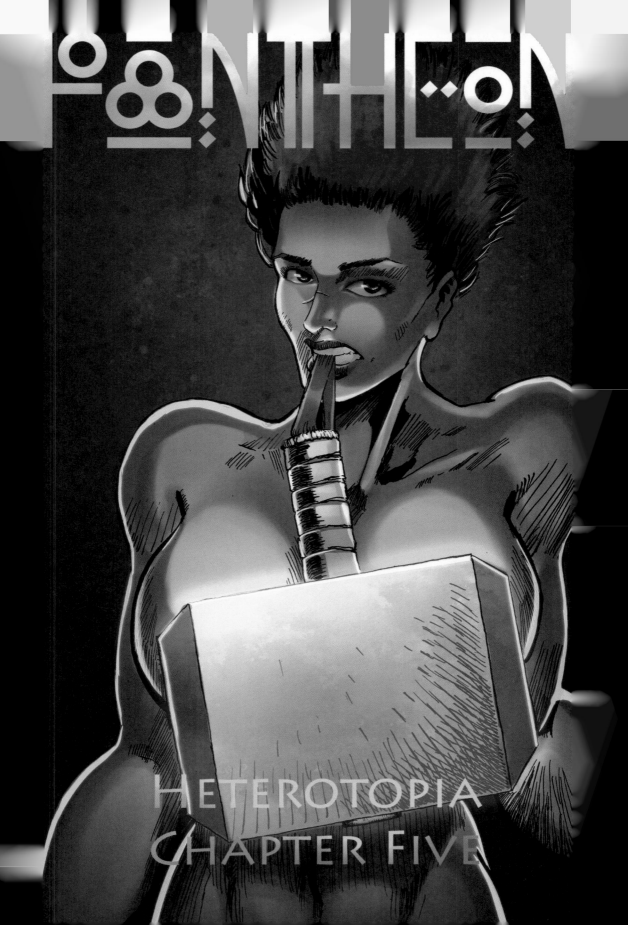

PANTHEON

HETEROTOPIA
CHAPTER FIVE

PANTHEON: HETEROTOPIA CHAPTER FIVE

A CHASE THROUGH SPACE & TIME, ACROSS INFINITY AND ETERNITY...
HURTLING DOWN TOWARD THE HEART OF THE MILKY WAY, PURSUED
BY THE ENIGMATIC HUNTER WHO RESISTS ALL EFFORTS BY THE
PANTHEON GODS TO THROW THE HUNTER OFF THEIR SCENT... WHAT
MAD GOLEM IS THIS? AND THEN A TERRIBLE EXPLOSION, AS REALITY
BURSTS ASUNDER IN A GREAT SHOWER OF SHARDS!

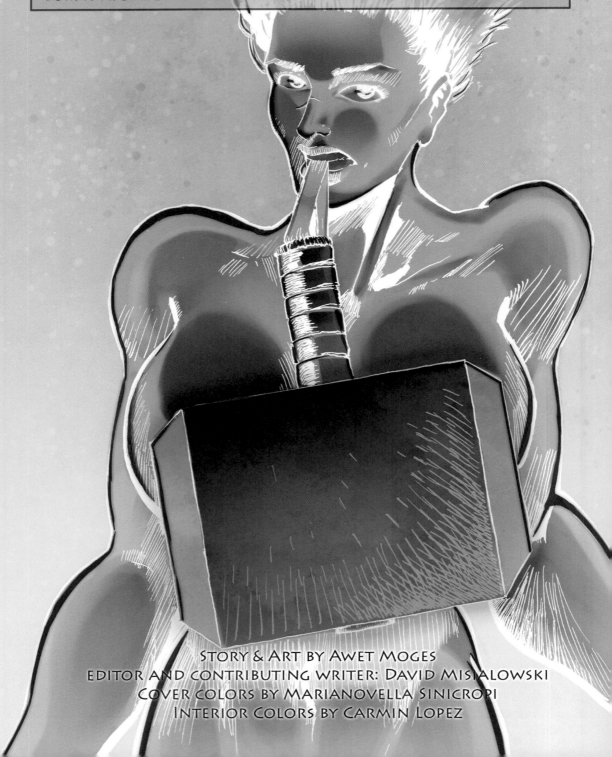

STORY & ART BY AWET MOGES
EDITOR AND CONTRIBUTING WRITER: DAVID MISIALOWSKI
COVER COLORS BY MARIANOVELLA SINICROPI
INTERIOR COLORS BY CARMIN LOPEZ

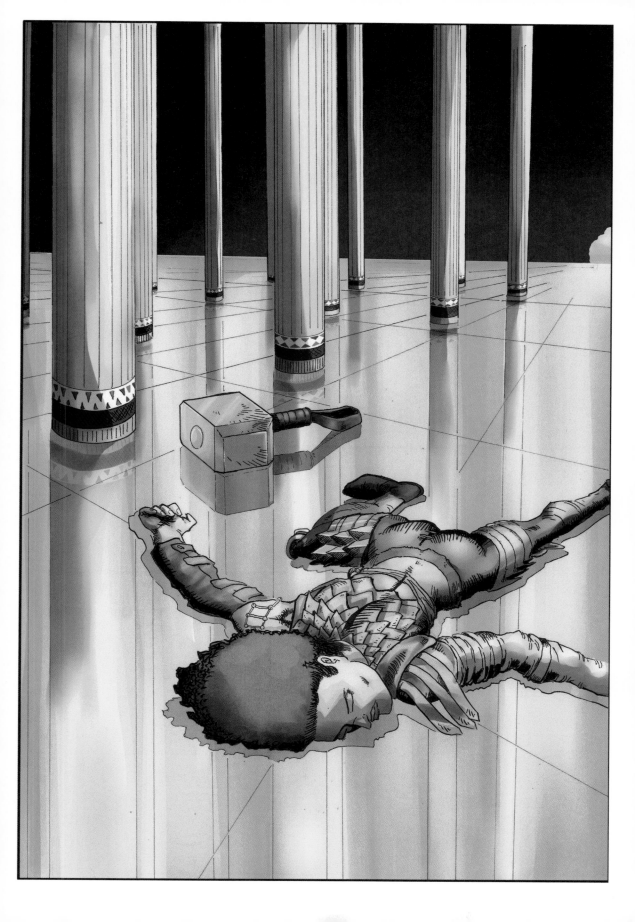

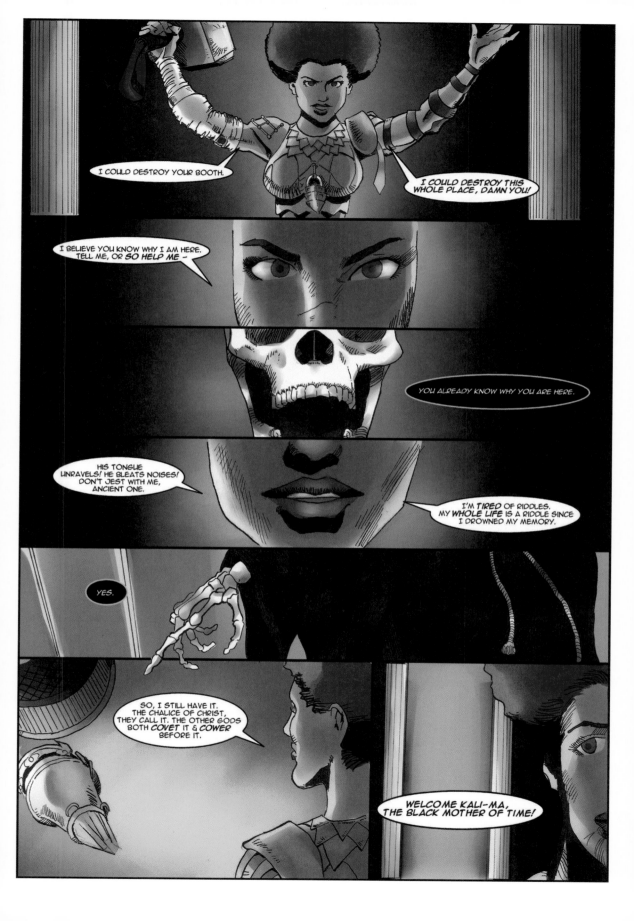

EPILOGUE

YES - I'M HERE. STRANGE...
YOU HAVE THE NEXUS TO THANK.
WHAT THE HELL JUST HAPPENED?
WE JUMPED THE INSTANT WE CROSSED THE EVENT HORIZON. DISORIENTATION USUALLY DISSIPATES WITHIN MINUTES.

ACKNOWLEDGMENTS

HI, **AWET MOGES** HERE. JUST ANOTHER DEAF ERITREAN-AMERICAN IMMIGRANT WHO GREW UP READING COMIC BOOKS AND MYTHOLOGY. **PANTHEON** IS THE END RESULT OF A THOUGHT EXPERIMENT WHEN I WAS ELEVEN YEARS OLD: WHAT IF THE GODS CONTINUED LONG AFTER OUR STORIES ENDED? IN OTHER WORDS, THIS GRAPHIC NOVEL IS A DECLARATION OF LOVE TO MYTHOLOGY AND ITS PHILOSOPHICAL CONTENT. WE HAVE NO TROUBLE EXPRESSING GRATITUDE FOR OTHERS, BUT I ALSO FIND IT ILLUMINATING TO GIVE THANKS TO WHAT IS DIFFICULT — THE THANKLESS YEARS SPENT IN SOLITUDE, RESEARCHING ARCANE KNOWLEDGE, DEVELOPING TECHNIQUES OF DRAWING, OBSTACLES AND FAILURES THAT TAUGHT ME RESILIENCE, AS WELL AS THE CRITICS WHO DID NOT BELIEVE IN ME.

BESIDES THE NECESSARY AMOUNT OF SWEAT, BLOOD AND TEARS, I OWE THANKS TO THE FOLLOWING:

MY PARENTS FOR RAISING ME RIGHT, PARTICULARLY FOR ALWAYS TAKING ME TO THE LIBRARY FOR STACKS AND STACKS OF BOOKS ON MYTHOLOGY AND EVERYTHING ELSE.

MY SISTERS **ZAID** AND **REZENET** FOR ENDLESS SUPPORT AND CHEERLEADING, BUT ALWAYS CAUTIONING ME FROM INDULGING IN THE MALE GAZE.

BILL HARKNESS FOR TELLING ME TO THROW THE LOG IN AND THE HELL WITH EVERYONE ELSE. **BARRY MCKAY** FOR SEEING THE POTENTIAL BEYOND THE FIRST DRAFT. **ELLIOT GREEN** FOR "POWER ELITE." **ERIK CALL** FOR PITCH-PERFECT ADVICE. **DARREN RUSSELL** FOR HIS BOTTOMLESS WELL OF KNOWLEDGE. **ROBERT AUGUSTUS** FOR HIS ENDLESS JOKES. AND THE REST OF THE **DEAF WRITERS' CLUB** FOR AMAZING FEEDBACK.

DAVID MISIALOWSKI FOR UNLOCKING THE GOD MODE OF **PANTHEON**. **SCOTT THORSON** FOR HIS FAITH AND INVESTMENT. AND THE BRILLIANT COLORISTS **SAJID MOHAMMED**, **MARIANOVELLA SINICROPI**, **NICOLE SERRA**, AND **CARMIN LOPEZ** FOR PUTTING UP WITH MY IMPOSSIBLE DEMANDS.

NOT TO MENTION AN EX-GIRLFRIEND FOR ERASING ALL THOSE PENCIL MARKS!

— LONG BEACH, CALIFORNIA, FEBRUARY 5, 2018

COMING

NOTE TO THE READER: THE WORK YOU HAVE JUST READ IS MERELY THE
OVERTURE TO THE SYMPHONIC POEM THAT IS PANTHEON, PRESAGING EPIC
ADVENTURES TO COME: JOURNEYS ACROSS THE MYTHOSCAPE, TO ALIEN
PLANETS WITH SENTIENT SPECIES FAR DIFFERENT FROM HUMANS, AND TO
THE UNDERVERSE AND OVERVERSE, REALMS THAT LIE ABOVE, BELOW AND
BEYOND THE REALM OF THE GODS. LOOK FOR LOVE AND WAR, BRAVERY
AND BETRAYAL, LUST AND ENVY, TERRIFYING ENCOUNTERS WITH CHAOS,
AND KAELI'S TITANIC CRESCENDO OF A BATTLE — WITH HERSELF.

SOON!

Printed in Great Britain
by Amazon